WALT DISNEY
PICTURES PRESENTS

P9-EED-829

DINOSAUR

I'm the FOTONOVEL,
the book which shows you
the entire movie,
from beginning to end.
Watch it over and over again.
I contain over 330 images
from this major Disney
production — plus original dialogue
from the film!

Keep me in your pocket,
or by your bed lamp.
Collect me — I'll be worth millions
when I grow old!
Well, maybe not millions. . .
But you can already find
my famous relatives on the Internet.

Check out my website: FOTONOVEL.COM
and meet us all

PLIO

ALADAR

NEERA

YAR

BAYLENE

EEMA

ZINI

KRON

BRUTON

Welcome to the
dawn of time.

Before the shadow of man
even walked the Earth,
giant dinosaurs
ruled the land.
And from those
early times,
only a few stories
have survived
into our days.

This is one of them . . .

Once upon a time, some 60 million years ago, there lived a brave iguanodon named Aladar.

Aladar's story begins before he is born, when he is still living in his egg. . .

4

. . . in his family's nesting grounds, a lush valley protected by strong, imposing mountains — Earth at its most primitive, unspoiled best. . .

... where the BIGGEST...

...and the Smallest of creatures co-exist in harmony.

6

On this particular balmy day, all is calm and peaceful. A large, gentle female iguanodon arranges her eggs with care when...

...something stirs her protective instincts. Sensing danger, she looks about with concern.

Suddenly, a massive, **HORRIFYING** carnotaur explodes through the dark forest wall, looking for his next meal.

Unwilling to abandon the nest, the mother iguanodon leans protectively over her eggs.

But when the carnotaur charges, she is forced to join the herd stampeding away, . . .

9

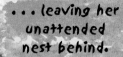
. . . leaving her
unattended
nest behind.

Spared from
the **HUGE**
trampling
feet of the
carnotaur,
only one egg
is left
miraculously
untouched.

But now, it is
alone and
vulnerable.

This fact is not lost on an opportunistic
oviraptor, who snatches it away and
races with it into the forest.

Later, under the green, lush canopy, the thief looks for a rock to break it on. But the egg is too tough; it won't crack!

SQUEEEEE

With a menacing another starving scavenger slaps the egg out of his grasp!

The greedy animal ends up dropping the egg into a swiftly moving river, hundreds of feet below.

11

Under the clear, fresh water, a sleepy labyrinthodont tries to swallow it but doesn't like the taste and spits it out.

12

A moment later, the egg is floating under the noses of two argumentative talaruras who miss it and can only watch it drift down stream. . .

. . .and into the perilous path of some pachyrhinosaurs.

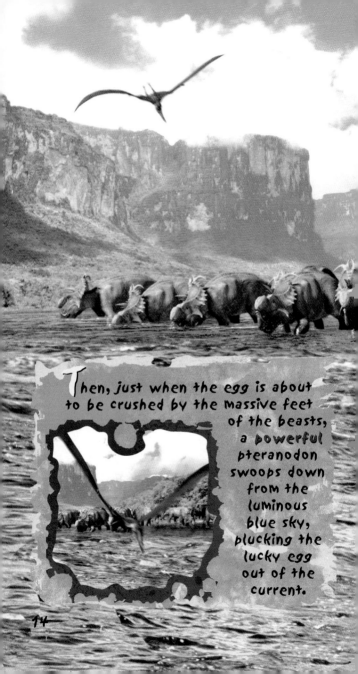

Then, just when the egg is about to be crushed by the massive feet of the beasts, a powerful pteranodon swoops down from the luminous blue sky, plucking the lucky egg out of the current.

14

With the prize safely clasped in her long, sharp beak, the pteranodon soars over a peaceful herd of dinosaurs grazing on a vast green plain.

With powerful flaps of her broad wings, the prehistoric bird transports the fragile cargo over deep canyons. . .

. . . and out over the open sea. . .

. . . far away,
to a beautiful,
idyllic island. . .

. . . where
her brood
of hungry
pteranodon
babies awaits
its next meal.

Suddenly the mother pteranodon is ambushed by a noisy flock of mischievous ichthyornis that tries to steal the egg.

Her grip loosens and the precious cargo plummets down, down into the green sea of forest.

17

The roof of soft leaves breaks the egg's fall. It lands on the mossy branch of a huge tree, miraculously intact.

There it sits, the lucky egg, in the silent cathedral of the virgin forest.

Some time later. . .

. . .a family of endearing, mysterious creatures called lemurs materializes through the thick vegetation.

After some hesitation, they decide to approach.

A particularly captivating pair of eyes peeks into the unusual scene, with keen curiosity. They belong to Plio, a beautiful female lemur.

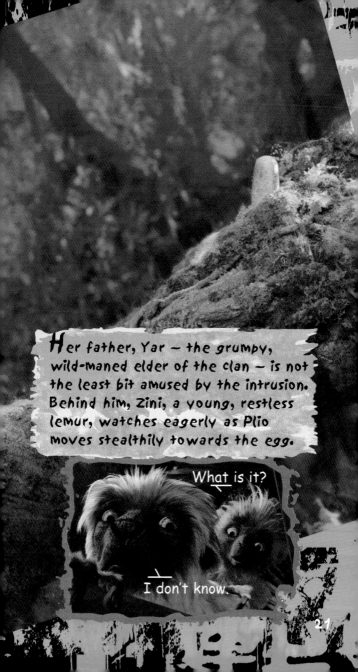

Her father, Yar — the grumpy, wild-maned elder of the clan — is not the least bit amused by the intrusion. Behind him, Zini, a young, restless lemur, watches eagerly as Plio moves stealthily towards the egg.

What is it?

I don't know.

To Plio, the egg is **enormous.**
She has never seen anything like it.
She creeps up as if drawn by a magnet.

Then suddenly....

CRACK!

A fissure appears
on the shell, and Plio
gently pries it open.

Plio, get
back here.
We don't
know what
it is.

She peeks at the gooey interior.

Dad, get over here!

Well, what is it?

At last, the baby iguanodon arrives in this primeval world. He sits comfortably in his half shell.

It's a cold-blooded monster from across the sea — vicious, flesh-eating.

24

It looks like a baby to me.

Babies grow up! You keep that thing, and one day we'll turn our backs and it'll be picking us out of its teeth!

25

So, what do
we do?

Get rid
of it.

I'm sorry,
little one.

Plio thrusts
the newborn
into her father's
uncertain hands.

Huh. . .?

All right!
I will! I'll do
it. I'll do it.
I'll show 'em...

Yar holds the baby
over the abyss. He
is about to drop him
to his death, but...

You better hurry up,
Dad. It looks hungry.

27

... the baby iguanodon opens his eyes...

... and Yar's resolve melts. He puts on a tough front, and hands the baby back to Plio.

Hmph — here... and watch his head!

29

Years later...

...a fully grown iguanodon runs through the pristine forest of Lemur Island, chasing terrified lemurs.

He corners two of the defenseless creatures and stares them down with his menacing reptilian eyes.

And then, in a flash. . .

...he swallows one of them whole!

SLUURP!

But then, PTOOEY! He spits the lemur out. It's all a game! They're just playing!

The menacing iguanodon is none other than Aladar, the baby dino who has grown into a *gigantic* member of the lemur clan.

The mischievous young lemur is Plio's daughter, Suri, a nimble female with a taste for practical jokes. She lands safely on a branch, drenched in dino-slobber.

That was GRRREAT!

Plio watches the playful antics with amusement...

A moment later, Aladar makes his way to the beach, looking for Zini.

The young lemur paces nervously. . .

Hey, sweetie, if you'll be my bride, I'll groom ya. Oh, that's good.

Girls, I am known as the professor of love, and school's in session.

Yeah, I still got it!

I hope it's not contagious.
I'm a raging epidemic of romance.
C'mon, hot stuff. You don't want to miss Yar's annual pep talk.

Oh, goody. . . I can't wait to hear the mating advice of an old monkey.
Hey, hey, hey. I heard that in his day that old monkey was quite a swinger.

As the warm, late afternoon sun bathes the Ritual Tree with its golden light, the young lemur males gather around Yar.

O.K. boys, gather 'round. Listen and learn from the master.

Now, girls, don't jump into the trees after the first boy with a cute backflip. It's more fun if you keep them guessing. . . .

And if a cute backflip doesn't work. . . guess!

You're never going to forget this day, so make it one to remember.

But. . . if you mess up, don't worry. They'll never remember.

Aladar is eager to get to the ceremony, and he comes to urge the boys on.

C'mon guys — we don't want to let 'em down.

Go on, now! Chest out! Chin up!

With that, the lemur boys jump onto Aladar's back, and off they go towards the canopy of the Ritual Tree.

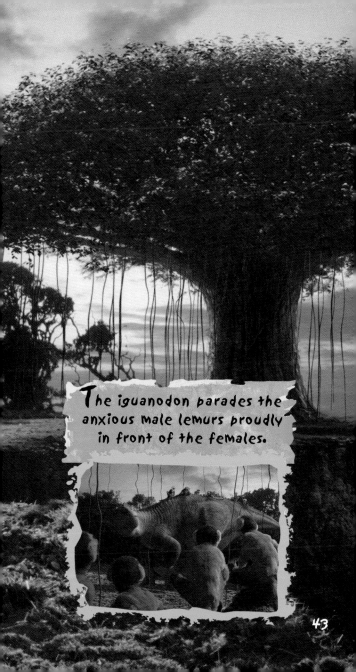

The iguanodon parades the anxious male lemurs proudly in front of the females.

Filled with teenage excitement, the boys leap from vine to vine with spectacular speed and agility.

AH-WHOOO

AHOOOGH

As the ritual ballet begins, the boys bellow, filling the sunset sky with their harmonious voices.

Well, almost. . .

The girls remain casual and aloof, practicing what Plio preached...

...making the boys work hard for attention.

All the lemurs in the grove are singing, swaying back and forth in a spontaneous, but instinctive ritual dance. The chanting grows and grows. Each girl climbs the vines and brings a flower...

...to her chosen beau.

46

One by one, the youngsters finally pair off, moving higher into the treetops.

Only Zini is left alone as he gets himself tangled in a vine, missing his chance to find a mate.

Aladar comes to offer Zini some much-needed moral support.

Aw, don't worry, Zini. You always have next year.

Hey, I'm lucky to be rid of them. With the ladies, before you know it, they all want to move to a bigger tree.

48

Ah, well. . . poor Zini. The clan still has one bachelor.

No. . . we have two.

Oh, Aladar, if only there were someone on the island for you — well, you know, who looks like you, but prettier.

Awww, c'mon, Plio. What more could I want?

Suddenly, Aladar is distracted and looks up at the sky. . .

WHOA!

. . . as several flashes of light streak toward the Earth.

The lemurs look on in amazement.

Dad. . .?

Something's wrong.

A shower of **FIERY** streaks fills the night sky.

Aladar, where's Suri?

She's up in the tree. . .

Aladar's voice trails off as an enormous fireball bursts through the sky with a frightening white glow.

As it comes closer and closer, terrifying the helpless clan of lemurs. . .

... the meteor disappears behind the horizon with a thundering roar.

A second later, the sky is flooded with a white light so intense that Aladar and the lemurs must shield their eyes.

But suddenly... night returns and everything becomes ominously quiet.

And then, with full force, the effect of the Fireball hits!

The island is shaken to its very foundations. The lemurs huddle together, aware that something awful has happened...

...when they hear...

...the SHOCK WAVE. A strange ghostly sound — like a phantom wind — terrifyingly shrill, and getting louder and louder.

The lemurs jump on Aladar's back as he storms into the forest . . .

Run, Aladar.
Run! Run!

. . . dodging the flaming debris crashing down from the sky.

Aladar dashes like a blur across a clearing, with the lemurs hanging on to his crest for dear life.

Not far behind, the wall of fire closes in, scorching everything in its path.

Suddenly the path ends at a sheer cliff, leaving their only escape a hundred feet down to the sea below.

But there is no time to hesitate. The advancing wall of fire is upon them!

58

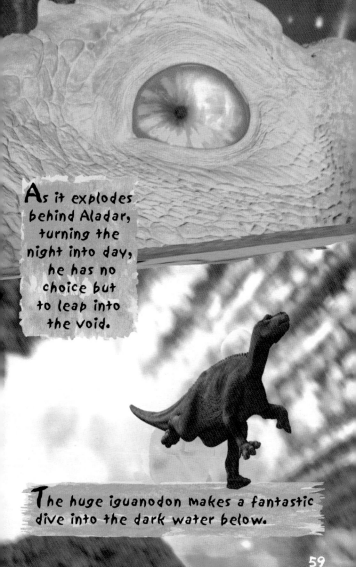

As it explodes behind Aladar, turning the night into day, he has no choice but to leap into the void.

The huge iguanodon makes a fantastic dive into the dark water below.

Moments later, he breaks back through the surface, gasping for air. Frantically, Aladar looks around for his lemur family and finds them clinging to floating debris.

Plio! Yar! Where are you?

He swims himself to exhaustion, but finally, his massive feet reach the dry Mainland. Here too, the Fireball has destroyed everything.

Aladar helps
the lemurs to
climb on his back
and together
they gaze with
sadness at the
island they once
called home.

Suri races to the water's edge, searching desperately for survivors.

They're all gone.

Shh, shhh. . . I'm here.

Aladar joins the lemurs and howls into the ash-filled wind. But the sea sends back no echo of hope.

They're all alone now . . . homeless and facing a dark, uncertain future.

After treading through arid, unknown territory, with the exhausted lemurs on his back, Aladar reaches a rocky plateau.

Aladar's attention is riveted to an odd-looking, slinky figure perched on high ground.

Everyone just be quiet.

As he moves through the gully, more of them appear.

Suddenly the creatures attack.

RAPTORS!!
Fast, clever and deadly with long rows of teeth, sharp as blades.

sssssss

65

Aladar tries desperately to run away. But the raptors close in by leaps and bounds, viciously chomping at his legs.

Their sharp claws and razor teeth cut through Aladar's thick hide, making him howl in pain.

AAHHH!

Still, Aladar bravely pushes on with his precious cargo, heading into what appears to be a sandstorm.

When Aladar least expects it, Kron, a massive iguanodon with burning eyes and a roaring voice, blasts out of the curtain of dust. . .

. . . pushing forward, knocking Aladar to the ground.

Stay out of my way!

The dust is thick as Aladar finds himself in the middle of a stampeding Herd.

He looks down to see a pack of unruly dino children scurrying through his legs. And, when he looks back up. . .

DONK!

Oww! Watch it!

Aladar wants to apologize, but he is speechless. He's just bumped into his first female iguanodon, and a beautiful one at that. She is Kron's sister, Neera.

Before he can give it more thought, a dark shadow covers them breaking the spell. The Earth shudders once again, and Aladar turns around to see . . .

... Baylene, a huge brachiosaur and Eema, a tired old styracosaur.

Walking backwards, huh? Well, let me know if that gets you there any faster.

The lemurs are amazed by the variety of sizes and shapes of the all the dinosaurs in the massive Herd.

WoW!

Look at all the Aladars. . .

Aladar can't believe his eyes. He's stunned — for this is the first time in his life he has seen creatures that look like him.

If you're even thinking of joining up. . .

Not far behind, the vicious raptors are set to pounce on the lemur family once again...

...but Aladar leaves them no chance as he bounds off down the bluff to join the dinosaur Herd.

As they make their way across the vast desert, Aladar — with his family on his back — wonders if he really belongs here.

At last, the Herd halts at the foot of a large hill.

There, Kron, the undisputed leader of the Herd, decides to make camp for the night.

We'll rest here for the night. Go on ahead, Bruton.

Kron, there is a more protected spot farther down the. . .

75

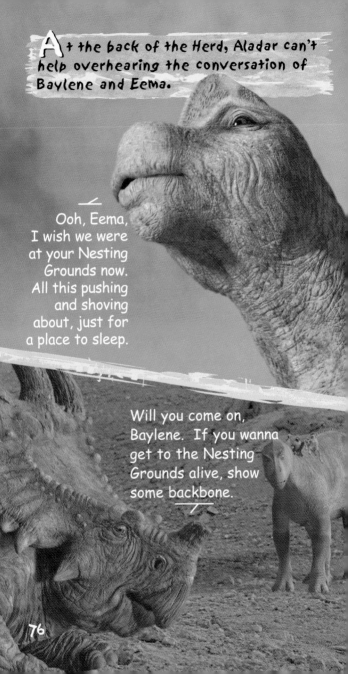

At the back of the Herd, Aladar can't help overhearing the conversation of Baylene and Eema.

Ooh, Eema, I wish we were at your Nesting Grounds now. All this pushing and shoving about, just for a place to sleep.

Will you come on, Baylene. If you wanna get to the Nesting Grounds alive, show some backbone.

Url, Eema's pet ankylosaur, greets Aladar.

Well, my word. Look at Url. He doesn't normally warm up to strangers so fast.

Baylene notices the lemurs on Aladar's back.

What an unfortunate blemish.

Excuse me?

77

My name's Aladar.
This is my family.
We're all that's left.

Oh, my dear,
I'm so sorry.

I heard you say
something about
Nesting Grounds.

It's the most beautiful place there is, child. It's where the Herd goes to have their babies. The hard job now is just getting there.

We are being driven unmercifully.

By whom?

Kron, the Herd's head honcho.

79

Just then three large figures emerge out of the gathering darkness — Kron, his sister Neera, and his lieutenant, Bruton.

Uh. . . excuse me, Kron? Got a second?

Get lost, kid.

Relax Bruton. Who are you?

Uh, Aladar. I was back here talking to these guys. . . they're having a hard time keeping up. So, you know, maybe you could slow down a bit?

Hmm. . .let the weak set the pace. . .now, there's an idea. Better let me do the thinking from now on, Aladar.

Hey, they need help back here!

Watch yourself, boy!

End of discussion. Kron moves ahead, but Neera lags behind, amazed by Aladar's boldness.

Don't worry, that's how my brother treats newcomers. . .no matter how charming they are.

And as Neera walks away...

Aladar, you sure know how to catch a girl's eye there, stud.

I wouldn't be catching nobody's eye if I was you — especially Neera's. You just mind what Kron tells you.

The next day, as dawn breaks, the Herd congregates at the edge of a vast desert.

Huh? Zini, what are you doing?

Hey, wake up. Enough with the beauty sleep!

I believe you left a wake-up call for the dawn of time. C'mon, move it!

What's the hurry?

Something's up. The Herd is gathering without us.

Rise and shine!
Kron says
everybody goes.

The charm
never stops
around here.

You say something?

Uh, no, no sir.

Unless you got a death wish, you and that little parasite better get moving.

Sheez, is that guy ugly or what?

Bruton moves off angrily. Aladar and Zini sigh in relief. And that's when Aladar notices . . .

. . . Neera with the orphans of the Herd up ahead.

Hey, hey, hey, Aladar. There's your girlfriend!

What are you talking about?

You know what I'm talking about. . . Neeeera. . . scaly skin, yellow eyes, big ankles? What you need is a little help from "The Love Monkey."

Oh, baby!

Neera and two baby dinos look back in surprise as Zini hides.

That, children, is what is known as a jerkasaurus.

And with that, the ice is broken.

Aladar chuckles through gritted teeth.

At dawn, the exhausted Herd gathers at the edge of a large desert. Bruton addresses them in a cold, trenchant voice.

If this is your first crossing, listen up! There is no water 'til we reach the other side. And you better keep up. . .

. . . 'cause if a predator catches you, you're on your own.

Oh my goodness, it looks like a very long walk.

Miles later, the Herd makes sluggish progress under an unmerciful sun. Yar rides comfortably on Eema's back.

Hey, old girl, you're wandering off a bit.

That's all I need. A monkey on my back!

Not far
behind,
a voracious carnotaur,
the biggest and most vicious
of all predators, picks up the
scent of the weary Herd.

*F*inally, Kron and Bruton look to the horizon with satisfaction. They bellow to the Herd to pick up the pace.

*H*earing the bellows, Eema becomes excited.

The lake!!

It's just over that hill, baby!

94

Then the Herd sees the dunes too.
Excitement spreads and the pace picks up.

A moment later
gasps of
disappointment
escape from their
dry throats.

They stare out at. . .
nothing. No water.
Just an enormous dry
lake bed of rocks and
the sunbaked bones
of a fallen dinosaur.

Maybe the rains collected somewhere else. What do you want us to do?

Take a scout and check the entire perimeter.

Bruton obeys, leaving Kron alone with his worries. Moments later, Neera approaches.

Kron, we've never gone this long without water. If we keep going, we'll lose half the Herd.

Then we save the half that deserves to live.

At the edge of the dry lake bed, Eema staggers in circles, disoriented and desperate for a drink of water.

We always had water. . . always! And plenty of mud.

Oh, Eema, please. The Herd won't wait. We must carry on.

Eema collapses in the dirt and Aladar strains to push her back on her feet.

You gotta get up!

There was water everywhere.

Baylene starts towards Eema when. . .

There is no water, dear.

. . . the ground gives way under her massive feet.

CRRRRAAAACK!

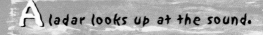
Baylene,
don't move.

Aladar and Zini
come over and start
digging around
Baylene's
huge foot.

Lift your foot,
Baylene. Now
press down.

Baylene lifts her delicate one-ton foot and. . .

Oh, what is it? What's wrong?

. . . steps on the ground again:

WATER!

A nice, big pool grows larger and larger around her foot.

Whoo hoo!! I always did like big girls!

Aladar bellows triumphantly to the Herd.

AOUUU!

Water! C'mon.

Aladar's excited voice reaches Neera and Kron.

He found water...?

That's it, Eema. Come drink.

Kron races down the hill and shoves Aladar aside.

Now, get out of the way!

103

The rest of the Herd rushes forward, pushing and shoving, trying to get to the water.

Wait. . .WAIT! There's enough for everyone!!!

Eema doesn't have the strength to get out of the way of the stampede.

EEMA!!

Aladar fights his way through the Herd to come to Eema's aid...

...as Neera watches from the ridge.

Meanwhile, Bruton and his scout arrive in a canyon.

Bruton, we've been walking in circles. There's no water here. I think we should get back.

Shhh! Keep it down. . . Let's get out of here.

Suddenly, two carnotaurs ~~attack!~~ The scout is dragged off by one of them. Bruton is chased up an embankment and barely escapes.

Back at the lake bed, as the Herd settles down for the evening...

...Suri tries to coax two dino kids out from a cave.

Come on! Come on out! No one's gonna hurt you.

Aladar calms the little ones down.

SLURP!

SLURP!

Take it easy — don't worry. Suri's just a hairball.

Neera has been watching Aladar from above and now approaches, trying to act casual.

You like kids, I see.

Well, the skinny ones can be a little chewy.
Neera laughs softly.
I'm Aladar — the. . . eh, jerkasaurus.
You're probably right.
Oh, sorry about that.

Plio watches Aladar and Neera.

Dad, look.

Huh?

Why did you help that old one?

What else could we do... leave her behind?

Neera just stares at Aladar evenly – and Aladar realizes with a jolt that she's serious. . .
Oh. You mean you actually. . .
Well, that happens all the time. You don't survive if you're not. . .

Strong enough?
Well, yeah.
Is that you talking? Or your brother?

Neera takes in Aladar's words. After a moment, he speaks to her in a deeply caring tone, as he begins to dig for water.

Look, Neera. If we watch out for each other, we all stand a chance of getting to your Nesting Grounds.

I'm not. But it's all I know. So, um. . . oh, water! Did you want some water?

Neera places her foot near Aladar's and presses down. Water appears and her foot slides... right into his.

Ooops...

Sorry...

No, you... you first.

Yar and Plio are still watching.

One down and. . .
well, one down.

Kron has also been watching. He is not
at all pleased with the growing friendship
between Aladar and his sister, Neera.

But then. . .

... a badly wounded Bruton approaches.

Kron... carnotaurs!

What? They never come this far north.

The Fireball must have driven them out.

You led them right to us! Maybe you can feed them with your hide! Move the Herd out double time!

Kron bellows loudly. The Herd begins to move out.

A **ladar and Neera hear Kron's bellows.**

What's happening?

My brother's
moving the Herd.

But, the others in
the back, they'll
never make it.

They'll slow
down the
predators.

You can't sacrifice
them like this!

120

Kron growls viciously and lashes out savagely at Aladar, knocking him down.

If you ever interfere again, I'll kill you.

Stay away from him!

Aladar. . . just go. I'll be okay.

121

A ladar gathers his friends and they make a valiant effort to keep up with the Herd, but no matter how hard they run, it's hopeless.

Come on, you guys. We're gonna get left behind. . . .

. . . Hurry up. We're losing them.

They continue to struggle, and Aladar can only watch as the Herd and Neera move off in the distance.

123

*H*ours later, as a
storm approaches. . .

. . . they are hopelessly far behind the rest of the Herd.

Oh, joy. . . blisters.

I got blisters on my blisters!

You don't wanna know where I got blisters.

Suddenly, a moan is heard.

What was that?

What's the worst thing it could be?

A carnotaur?

Okay, what's the second worst thing it coud be?

Two carnotaurs! Oh, my goodness!

That's it — I'm gone.

127

They climb up a hill to see it's Bruton, crippled by his wounds.

Oh, what happened?

Carnotaurs. . . ! We should keep moving.

Hey, uh, you don't look so good. Let me help you.

Save your pity. I just need some rest. Now, get away from me.

Suit yourself. If you change your mind, we'll be in those caves.

Aladar and his friends take shelter from the rain which has begun to fall.

It's dark, but at least it's dry.

I like dry. It's the dark part I'm having trouble with.

Baylene turns to look toward the cave entrance.

We appear to have a visitor.

It's Bruton. Aladar goes outside the cave to help him in.

What is it with you?

Least I know enough to get in out of the rain. Now come on.

Uh, you can lie down with us. It's warmer.
Bruton moves off and lies down away from them.
May I remind you that he's one of them?
Well, looks like he's one of us now.

P lio finds a small, spiky plant, which she breaks open to release a thick, gooey liquid. She applies the liquid to Bruton's wounds. He grunts in relief.

This plant grew on our island. It will make you feel better.

Why is Aladar doing this. . . pushing them on with false hope?

It's hope that's gotten us this far.

Later that night...

...Bruton and Aladar are awakened by approaching figures.

Sssshhh! Carnotaurs.

What do we do?

Wake the others.

A flash of lightning floods the cave, exposing Aladar.

The carnotaurs waste no time. One bites Aladar's tail and proceeds to drag him across the cave.

And just as the two carnotaurs are about to kill him . . .

. . . Bruton pushes them aside, saving Aladar.

ROAR!!

I'll hold them off.
Save yourself.

ARRRRR!!

Aladar hesitates, but finally goes to help the others.

Bruton looks toward a pillar and comes to a decision.

He runs, smashing into the pillar. The roof of the cave begins to collapse, crushing both a carnotaur and Bruton in the falling debris.

— Bruton!

The dust clears and Aladar digs away the rocks to find Bruton — dead.

Bruton. . . No!!!

As they realize the heroic sacrifice Bruton made to save them, Aladar and his friends slowly back away from the dangerous pile of shifting rocks. And, on the other side. . .

. . . the surviving carnotaur exits the cave.

139

Meanwhile, the Herd is having trouble with its trek.

The two orphan children struggle to keep up. One of them collapses as the oblivious and uncaring Herd continues forward.

All looks bleak, until. . .

... before them appear the legs of a member of the Herd....

It's Neera. She helps them to their feet...

It's okay, little ones. We're going to make it.

... and, with a look to the Herd — now so far ahead — she slowly walks along with the two children.

Back at the cave, Aladar and his friends have reached a dead end. Their path is blocked. There's nowhere else to go.

I guess we just go back.

Zini senses something in the air.

Sniff

Sniff

Sniff

Hold on a moment. Do you smell that?

Sniff

Yeah!

Zini and Suri scamper ahead, following the scent and discover...

...a thin shaft of light.

Good show.

Get a load of that.

Aladar moves up to the wall and begins to push. But just as beams of light shine through...

Everybody, stand back! We're outta here.

...the wall collapses, blocking the tiny opening.

Noooo!!!

144

Something in Aladar snaps.

Consumed by frustration, he flails at the uselessly before slumping down against a rock in defeat.

We're not meant to survive.

145

They are all stunned to hear this from Aladar. He turns away from them, but Baylene storms over with uncharacteristic **ANGER.**

Oh, yes we were! We're here aren't we? Shame on you!

The worst of it is, you allowed an old fool like me to believe I was needed. And do you know what? You were right. I, for one, am not willing to die here.

And with that, she marches over to the wall and begins pushing with all her might.

One by one, the others join in, struggling in vain against the rock wall. Aladar finally joins them and they all push together until...

CRACK

...the wall comes tumbling down...

. . . and daylight comes streaming into the cave.

Oh, dear. . .

Before them is a stunningly beautiful mountain-ringed valley.

The Nesting Grounds. . . It's. . . It's untouched.

They rush down the hill, laughing joyously.

Baylene plunges into the lake.

Cannonball! Wahoo!

Amateur!!

Not bad, but I don't get it. Where's the Herd?

Not to mention Neera.

They'll get here. . . soon. . . enough. . .

Oh, no. I spoke too soon.

*E*ema sees a huge landslide blocking the entrance to the valley.

What is it?

That is the way we used to get in here.

Aladar sees the obstruction. . .
They'll never make it over that!
. . . and turns to go back for the Herd on the other side.
Aladar, wait, wait. . . Kron'll eat you alive.
Let him try!!
Oh! I hope Kron's in a listening mood.

On the other side
of the avalanche,
the Herd finds the
path into the valley
is obstructed.

Kron looks
up at the
wall of rock
and thinks
a moment.

We'll find
a way
around it.

No, we
climb it.

Neera stares at him, stunned.

Meanwhile, Aladar pushes his way through the cave...

...and narrowly avoids the carnotaur.

Kron and the Herd try climbing the rockslide.

Our survival, our future is over these rocks. Now let's go home!

Stop! I've been to the valley! There's a safer way.

Aladar appears.

Where? Straight to the carnotaurs?

If we hurry, we can get around them. You can't get over those rocks. You're gonna kill the Herd! Now follow me!

Kron charges at Aladar. . .
They're staying with me!
. . . attacking him and knocking him to the ground.
But Aladar fights back, holding his own.

Kron raises his spike at Aladar, but he's suddenly broadsided.

He turns toward what hit him and is shocked to see that it is his sister.

Neera!

Neera moves away to help Aladar. Together they head out, followed by the Herd. Neera ignores Kron.

But they hear a bellow, and a carnotaur appears in the path. It runs toward the herd, which begins to panic.

ROAR!

Don't move! If we scatter, he'll pick us off! Stand together!

The carnotaur charges. . .

. . . but Aladar bellows right back.

ROAR!

Soon the rest of the Herd follows suit, bellowing all together.

ROARR

ROAR

The carnotaur becomes disoriented. . .

. . . and the Herd moves right past, around a turn in the path.

Kron, meanwhile, struggles to climb the rockslide. The carnotaur's attention shifts to the lone figure of Kron, and starts moving toward him.

Kron turns to see the carnotaur coming toward him.

Kron!

Neera runs to help.

Kron looks down and realizes the cliff is too steep to maneuver.

He turns back around to see the approaching carnotaur.

No...

ROAR!

... and finds the inner strength to confront the beast.

The carnotaur bites Kron by the neck, bringing him to the ground.

But as the carnotaur is going in for the kill...

...Neera rushes over and pushes it away. Aladar joins the fight. Then...

...the carnotaur's own weight causes the rocks to crack. The beast falls to its death below. Aladar barely manages to climb to safety.

Neera turns her attention to her brother, but it's too late.

Kron. . .

Aladar comforts her.

Sometime later...

. . . an egg
moves. . .

167

... and begins to hatch.

Look! Somebody wants to meet you.

An adorable baby iguanodon peers out.

169

Not far away, Zini is flanked by a group of obviously smitten female lemurs.

Hey, look what I found! New neighbors! Any of you ladies up for a game of "Monkey in the Middle?"

Ah-Whooo!

Aladar laughs and starts to bellow...

170

. . . the Nesting
Grounds. . .

. . . where life
goes on and on
and on . . .

The
End.